Evincepub Publishing

SMIG - 65, Parijat Extension, Bilaspur, Chhattisgarh 495001

First Published by Evincepub Publishing 2017

ISBN: 978-1-5457-1050-0

Never or Forever

IT IS YET AN ENIGMA

Sajal Jain

About the Author

Sajal jain is a young author, poet and presently a student of engineering in UIT, RGPV, Bhopal Madhya Pradesh. He was born in Sagar, Madhya Pradesh and brought up in Jabalpur, Madhya Pradesh. This book is his first work as an author. His poem writing is usually based on his real life incidents, this book is the outcome his deep thoughts and beautiful imagination. His writing always emphasize on how to keep any relation forever. He also writes on moral ethics and on some of the natural elements of human behaviour such as happiness, hope and expectations. And, the inspiration behind his writing is his best friend Ayushi tiwari.

About the Book

It is a short fiction love story which gives you different definitions of love. A love is not always about achieving the person whom you love but sometimes its about going out of the way and do anything for the happiness of the person whom you love. Story is about loving someone without expecting a love & togetherness in return. It is about the purity of that friendship in which even though girl didn't love the boy still she cares and concerned for the happiness of boy because of his niceness. Its about the thin layer between hope & expectations and if one should keep theirself in that layer then he or she could be happiest person in the world. It is about the inner beauty of the girl that make any boy to do heart tickling efforts just for her happiness. Incidents of the story will always keep you connected with the story, book is fully decorated with some cute heart touching incidents, motivational quotations and poems by author through out the story.

Dedication

DEDICATED TO THE

BEST PART OF MY LIFE...!!

Acknowledgement

Well, to say that this book is mine will be not be true. At best, it was just my imagination. There are some wonderful people in my world, who made my imagination and thoughts to take form of this beautiful book which you are holding in your hand. I would like to thank all of them and in particular;

Rishabh Bagora, Abhiuday Singh and Mohammad Afzal who provided me with the system for preparing the manuscript, without them it was never possible to complete the manuscript on time.

Sonal Baraskar and Shikha Singh who had done all the correction work in the manuscript. A big thanks to them because the correction process consumed their lot of time still they had done it .

Kirti Barman and Prachi Harshey for such an amazing title of the book

Shiv Pratap Singh and Ayushi Tiwari for designing the beautiful front cover for the book and back text that is beautiful poem written by Ayushi Tiwari.

Atishi tiwari, Shiv Pratap Singh, Rishabh Bagora, Prachi Harshey, Sonal Baraskar,Soumya Nema, Riyansha Khatri, Sonal Gonge,Palak thareja and Rounak Singh – amazing friends who read the manuscript and gave honest reviews. All of them also stayed with me through out the entire process.

Abhishek Singh for the suggestions through out the process.

My family members – Prakash Jain, Vijay Jain, Sangeeta Jain and Shobhna Jain who has always supported me and allowed me for this work.

This is a work of fiction, but fictions needs real inspiration and that inspiration for me comes from my Best friend – Ayushi Tiwari who was the first one to read the complete manuscript. Thanks to her for always being the inspiration behind my writing and being the real cause behind the book.

Some names are repeated it shows how crucial role they had throughout the entire process of the book and one of the name from them who helped a lot at the every stage of the process, is Sonal Baraskar, so a special thanks to her.

The editor and the entire team of Evincepub Publishing Team for being so professional and friendly in the process.

This book was not possible without the support of all these peoples so once again a very big thank you to all of them and love them all a lot.

Content Table

Chapter 1

Love At First Sight

It was the very first day of the school after the summer vacations. The students were back on the track of school life after having an enjoyable vacation. There were the excitement and happiness on everyone's faces as they were meeting their school friends after a long time. Everyone was busy sharing their vacation experiences; some went to their grandparents, some went for family trips & some stayed at home spending their leisure by playing video games, T.V., cricket etc.

The hustle bustle was still there when a sudden noise came, a kind of storm which actually was the signal of Ashutosh Sharma's presence and there he entered the class. Ashutosh Sharma, a tall, muscular guy, who just loved to trouble people, especially girls. His only job was to tease them with funny names, and thus had an image of a bad boy in front of them. Girls often hated him & used to fight with him.

Ashutosh had a group of 5 friends; Arush, Sameer, Rohit, Shekar and Ashutosh himself. As soon as he entered the class, he immediately joined his group as he had some fresh gossips for them. "BHAI LOG, there's a new admission in our class and that too a girl and she's damn hot man. She is from St. Xavier School" he said with an excitement. But no one actually bothered much about his word except the one guy that was Arush. Arush was a simple & innocent boy, a studious one, always engaged with his books and always maintained a distance with girls; entirely opposite of Ashutosh.

But Usually Arush was least interested in talks related to girls, but that day was different. Those words of Ashutosh stuck into his mind and he started imagining that girl, then there was a complete silence in the class and then his imagination, "THE BEAUTY APPEARED". There the new girl entered in IX- B. Her entry was catchy or maybe her beauty made it. Everyone started staring at her. She was much more beautiful than what Arush imagined. "I have never seen someone so beautiful. Her adorable eyes and that spark in them, her short height, fair complexion, and that cuteness made her much more beautiful" he thought. These thoughts were unexpected for him but he was helpless, he couldn't stop them. A girl in regular school uniform having two plaits with ribbons in them seemed like an angel for him. He didn't want to move his eyes off her, but unfortunately, he had to.

Arush wondered "Is this what they call LOVE AT FIRST SIGHT?" This phrase was new for him, as for him such things sounds good only in movies and dreams. "Arush Agrawal is in love with that girl?" he asked himself and then answered "Impossible, I can only fall in love with my books and studies." And then finally he removed all those thoughts from his mind and came back to his normal life. Then Ashutosh told the group, the name of that beauty was Ishika Malhotra. They both went to the same coaching which was the reason why he had all this information.

The day then passed with the usual school routine, but turned to be special for Arush. 21st June 2011, when he saw the love of his life.

———————— ◆ ————————

"If I knew I would be falling in love with this angel, I would have searched for her harder and found her sooner", was the only thought going on his mind".

Chapter 2

Conversation With His Own Mind

The next day Arush went to school, things were a bit different from his daily routine, he was having some strange feelings or butterflies in his stomach as his eyes were looking for someone, they were searching Ishika in that crowd. Even though he had convinced himself that liking or loving a girl wasn't meant for him, he couldn't stop. It was his mind that was convinced, but his heart was still waiting for her. Then the wait was over as she entered the class and his heart got a huge relief. That one sight of her filled him with happiness.

With each passing day, his affection towards Ishika grew even more. His eyes looked for her only all the time and now his heart wanted even more. He wished to gain her attention to have a conversation with her. Till now he had realised that he has started liking her, but he decided to keep his feelings to himself and never shared them with anyone.

Ishika initially had a reserve nature as she was new but by now she had made herself comfortable in the new school, new class, new environment and had made new friends. Not only girls, but she was interacting with boys as well, which was now making Arush insecure. He

4

wished he could approach her, but his shy nature resisted. On the other hand, Ashutosh had started troubling her as well by teasing her with different funny names. Arush felt jealous as at least Ashutosh can talk to her but he couldn't.

Ashutosh was a brilliant student, so Ishika at times referred him for his doubts and sheets of the coaching. At those moments, Arush too wished to be a part of that coaching, because in that way he might have had a chance to talk to Ishika and then she might had preferred him for her doubts.

It was not only Ashutosh who made Arush insecure, but there was another guy named Ishmit, who was a problem for him. Ishmit was the one who was over friendly with girls. He could easily become friends with girls and always made a try on beautiful girls. But then somehow Arush came to know, Ishika was not at all interested in him which gave him a relief.

Even though Ishika was not at all interested in those boys, still Arush found them lucky as they could at least talk to her and Arush was still waiting for his first conversation with her. He couldn't figure out how to initiate a conversation with her or what she will think if he messed up or what will others think if he'll talk to her. He wanted to make his first impression perfect. He wondered whether she knows his name or has ever noticed his existence. All these thoughts were not allowing him to talk to her.

Chapter 3

Reason Of That Smile (Dream Came True)

As the days passed, Arush's feelings for Ishika grew stronger but still, he was waiting to have his first interaction with her. And finally, the day came when for the first time she noticed him. It was the maths class after the lunch break; teacher gave some problems on the board and asked everyone to solve them. Also, if someone was interested he or she could solve it on the board as well. And because of coaching, Ashutosh and Ishika was expert in mathematics so definitely knew the solution. It was Ishika who took the stand and went to solve the question on board. While she was doing so, Ashutosh was passing comments continuously which made her angry. Ashutosh was sitting beside Arush, so when Ishika turned around to look she thought it was Arush. This was the first time she noticed him, but this not how Arush wanted it to be.

For him it was a mixed feeling now, as he was happy that Ishika noticed him, but at the same time worried because he didn't want her to think he too was a trouble making guy like Ashutosh. His mind was constantly asking for her opinion about him. Thereafter, Arush started doing weird things in the class in order to gain her attention, to make her notice him and finally once again he succeeded. He was sitting on the last bench singing the famous song of that time "WHY THIS KOLAVERI D..." in a funny tone and loud enough that it was audible to Ishika. She turned eagerly to know whose funny voice was that and noticed Arush, & smiled. This was for the first time she smiled, because of Arush. Maybe she found him crazy and was smiling on his craziness, but that too made him happy as he always wished to be the "REASON BEHIND HER SMILE."

Days passed and Arush kept trying to gain attention of Ishika. Then one day, they both were sitting in the same row and something happened which made Arush tease Ishika by the name of Ishmit. But she didn't like it and Arush could see that on her face, he immediately said sorry. "SORRY" was the first word, said by him to her. Then he thought of doing something stupid to change her mood. It was Hindi class, teacher was giving the grammar lessons while she said "KARTA NE SWAYAM KARYA KIA," just to explain the phrase, and Arush suddenly replied "SWAYAM NE KYU KIA WHY NOT SHARON". This made Ishika burst into laughter and Arush's plan worked. Later they had a little conversation about the TV show D3 as Swayam and Sharon were its characters. This was the first interaction between them, which started with a sorry and ended with smile on both the faces.

Another day, turned to be bad for Ishika which made Arush's day worst. Ishika met with an accident on the way to the school. She got some serious injuries, her knee was bleeding badly, and elbow was injured. When

Arush came to know about this, he immediately went to the primary wing to get the first aid box and also called Ishika's friends so that they could take the first aid box to her. The teachers and her friends took good care of her and gave her the proper treatment. But she was still sniffing with pain. Arush could feel the same pain or even more as he just couldn't do anything to reduce it or to share it.

For next few days, Ishika didn't come to school. She was on a leave for the recovery. But Arush was missing her. He was missing her beautiful eyes, innocent face, those lips which never stopped and kept on talking, her hairs which always fall on her pretty face and everything. He was missing her presence around him badly. And after some days finally she was back which brought a huge smile on Arush's face.

———— ◆ ————

"Isn't it amzing how an unknown person turns to be the reason of your happiness and with time every small thing related to them makes you happy? You cry in their pain and feel on the cloud nine when they are happy."

Chapter 4

Beauty With Brain

For next few months, there was no interaction between Ishika and Arush. As Ishika was always engaged with her assignments, so Arush stopped approaching her because they have their summative assignment examination in upcoming months, so both of them needed to focus on studies.

Arush worked hard for examination but as till class 8th Arush was good enough in mathematics so he didn't give much time to it. He took mathematics lightly but this time mathematics dominated over Arush's knowledge. When he saw the question paper he was shocked to see the level of question paper as it was quite tough one for him. But Arush thought that paper was really tough so it will be going to be tough for the whole class but when result came, a different picture was there in front of Arush.

Whole class was worried because of mathematics. All the copies were shown, most of the students in the class got expected marks but when Arush got to know about highest, it was 90 out of 90. It was Ishika, the Ishika Malhotra. Then 89 by Ashutosh and 81 by Ayesha. These were the only ones who got marks in 80's in mathematics. That moment was the disappointing moment for Arush, but he was surprised too that they can score such an outstanding marks in such a tough paper. But then he reminded himself that all three of them were from coaching where they had a brilliant tutor. That is why even the so tough paper of mathematics was the simple one for them. Arush never felt so small in his life. He was feeling like a beggar hanging out with Kings. See, being bowled on a Yorker doesn't affect you that much but on a full toss does. Same was the case with Arush this time. Maths was the full toss for him because he loved the subject.

Additionally, Arush was also worried about what Ishika will think about him now if she will get to know about his marks. Well, we can say he was probably more worried about this only. On one hand, she got full marks and Arush was not even around her. Even though, she never noticed Arush or his marks but still that was his hope which was making him concerned of it. According to Arush's perception, Ishika was a girl who will demand for moonlight and Arush was trying to impress her with a lamp.

Arush really felt ashamed that day and realized that he had no match with Ishika whether it's about looks, knowledge or marks. In every field she was one step ahead of Arush. But, to make a match with her in studies, Arush need to work hard because somehow Arush thought that she was a bright student so she would never like an average student like Arush. As Arush wants his result to be remarkable enough so that atleast it could grab attention of Ishika.

For Ishika, Arush was just a name of her classmate. But for Arush, Ishika was the only reason of his happiness & now she was even his inspiration for studies because Arush was in love with Ishika. Of course, teenage love is one of the purest forms of love. It's selfless love, with no dirty needs, just a desire and a dream to be with your partner.

———◆———

Chapter 5

Accomplished Goals

Now it was tough time. Arush had six months to work on his mathematics and this time he was determined that for next six months he will only focus on his studies. It was a tough task for him but he had a mindset that if he will score good marks then only he will reach upto a level from where he could stole his girl's attention.

He started working on his mathematics, referred extra books other than the syllabus books and apart from it, worked on his other subjects equally as well. These six months passed quickly and exams were near. Finally, a day came when he had to give output from all the input that he had taken from last six months.

It was the mathematics exam, Arush was quite nervous because the previous one was disastrous for him. This time the paper was tough enough as expected but, Arush was prepared for such a paper, it went passed quite smoothly and this time it was a better one for Arush.

Now again, it was the time for results, Arush was nervous before seeing his marksheet but after seeing his marksheet there was huge happiness on his face implying the success of his hard work and he shouted with excitement "YEAH I HAVE DONE IT!".

Arush got 92% in his results, marks were not mentioned in the marsheet as copies were outside the school for correction, but Arush got excellent grades in mathematics and this time his marks were around Ishika, Ishika got 94% marks.

Now they all were promoted to class 10th, a crucial one in every student's life as it is always asked for the marksheet of class 10th & 12th. Arush wanted to do his best in the results of 10th board and he started working for it from the very beginning of the academic session because it was Arush's personal opinion, that if he will do well in boards that there will be chance to be highlighted in his school. Arush never bothered for the whole school but he wanted to grab Ishika's attention. He wants Ishika to notice him and that was only possible if he manage to do well in his board examination.

But the way class 10th was not that simple, he needs to give equal time to all of his subjects and secondly, there were many distractions too. As Ishika had completed his one year in the school, now she was known to the whole school and her beauty was the hottest topic for whole school. She was the 'DIVA' of the class and also one of the most beautiful, prettiest and cutest girls of the school. So, it was quite obvious that Arush was not only one who likes Ishika, there was long queue for Ishika. Some were classmates of Ishika and some were the seniors. This was the part of insecurity for Arush and somehow an obstacle in the way of his studies.

Even though Arush was not even her friend still he had insecurities like a typical boyfriend for Ishika but these insecurities were within Arush only as he never told anyone about his feelings in the class.

Some positive things too happened in his academic life. At the start of session, they ,got a new mathematics teacher & coincidently, he was the one who previously checked the copies of the mathematics of Arush's class. He was called at the stage for his introduction and during his introduction he told that he was the one who checked copies of class 9th 'B'. The teacher was very much impressed with the copies of 4 students; Ashutosh, Arush, Ishika and Ayesha and asked everyone to give huge round of applause for them. That was pride and confidence enhancing moment for Arush, because Arush was the only one in 4 of them who had done it without coaching.

Things were going well from the studies point of view for Arush, but that obstacle comes into act for Arush because now Ashutosh & Ishika were getting closed to each other. It sounds filmy that the boy, who never missed the single chance to trouble a girl, suddenly starts liking her. Well Arush was pretty sure that Ishika is never going to like Ashutosh as they had so many serious fights in the past.

But life is unpredictable, you never know what will happen in the very moment of your life and it always let you meet the most unexpected things and same thing happen with Arush. Ishika and Ashutosh had exchanged their contact numbers and they started chatting on calls and messages till 4 am according to Ashutosh. Ashutosh usually use to tell about his chats with Ishika to his group that simply breaks Arush.

Unfortunately, Arush had no other choice left as no one else was aware about Arush's feelings.

Well things were not end here, as Ashutosh was audacious enough to sit beside Ishika on her seat that was strange because boys and girls were not supposed to sit together on the same seat in the class. But soon it turned to be usual scene of the class & they used to talk for hours and having great time with each other. All these things were raising Arush insecurities & hurting him badly but he was helpless at the moment, he couldn't do anything even for himself.

But soon Arush realized that he had lost Ishika, even though he never own her, they were not even friends but still there was a nostalgic feeling of losing someone very special. Arush too considered things in positive manner, as Ishika was happy with Ashutosh and her happiness was his priority, so he decided to be happy.

Ashutosh and Ishika were similar in many respects as both of them were brilliant students and on the other hand Arush was still struggling for better results of boards, whereas Ashutosh and Ishika were looking to crack some of the national level examinations, such as NTSE and KVPY. With all these thoughts, Arush concluded himself that there was a huge difference between Arush and Ishika. Ishika was a fancy girl to whom every boy wants to assimilate & Arush was simple boy with whom no girl would even prefer to talk.

Thereafter, Arush decided to focus only on his studies and he was doing well too but somehow interaction of Ishika and Ashutosh had disturbed him badly. He turned to be a silent person and then he didn't used to talk much with anyone in the class. May be He was trying to hide his feelings behind his silence.

Now Arush tried to keep his writing work and school assignments up to date in the hope that if in case Ishika's work will be incomplete then she may refer the notebook of Arush for the completion of her work. It sounds stupid but cute too, its love which is beyond all stupidity & craziness.

The plan of keeping the work complete worked and Ishika asked Arush for his Hindi notebook. Finally, a happy moment for Arush after long time. He immediately gave his notebook to her and on very next day, she returned it with a thanks.

The class of Hindi was going on, Arush took out his Hindi notebook from the bag and suddenly a photograph falls from his notebook, Ashutosh noticed it, there was a cute, healthy girl child in the photograph. Ashutosh picked it up and asked the Hindi teacher to announce about the photograph so that the one who owns the photograph can take it back. As Hindi teacher announced about the photograph, Ishika immediately shouted with concern "MERI HAI, MERI HAI", whole class turned towards Ishika and Ashutosh quickly responded her "TERI PHOTO ARUSH KI COPY ME KYA KAR RAHI HAI?" Whole class burst into laughter that was embarrassing moment for Ishika and soon her embarrassment turned into tears and she started crying. Arush felt guilty since just because of him she was crying. Arush always wish to be the reason of her happiness but now he was the reason behind her tears.

Actually, that was not Arush's fault, may be in her home when Ishika was completing her work that photograph came in the notebook of Arush by mistake.

One day Ishika went to class 10th A, a class with full of naughty boys, most of them were friends of Ashutosh and they knew about Ashutosh and Ishika. So when Ishika entered their class they started teasing her with the name of Ashutosh, when she came back her face was red with anger & frowned too. She angrily warned Ashutosh that she really didn't like such kind of stuffs, so it will be better if such kind of incidents will not repeat in the future again. That moment Arush decided that he will never going to confess his feelings to Ishika, if it will make her face such stuffs in the class, after all, for Arush happiness and comfort zone of Ishika was much more important than his feelings. So he will not be going to make her feel uncomfortable because of his feelings.

Ishika had passed almost one and half year in the school, and Arush yet not had proper interaction with Ishika, now he decided to take an initiative, he can't be her special friend but atleast he decided to try to become her friend.

———— ◆ ————

Chapter 6

"Shayad Wali Friendship"

Now Ishika's birthday was near, which was an opportunity for Arush to initiate the thread of friendship with Ishika but unfortunately, that was a holiday on 10th November. This again made him sad and he had to dropout his plan.

But this time Arush was determined. He had planned to give Ishika her favorite chocolates on the working day before her birthday. At first, he thought of giving her directly but then he thought this might embarrass her or her friends will tease her or she might find this strange. So, he secretly kept them in her bag with a "HAPPY BIRTHDAY" note without mentioning his name.

Apart from putting those chocolates, he asked Aditi to wish her from his side as well. Aditi was Rohit's sister who was Arush's best friend. She was the only girl in the class with whom Arush was comfortable and can talk freely. Also, Aditi was Ishika's neighbour so she would wish her on her birthday for Arush.

Arush also decided to take help from Aditi to be a friend of Ishika. He finally gathered courage and told her how much he likes Ishika and wanted to be a friend of her, so he will need her help for this. Aditi smiled and agreed to help him. Ishika's birthday passed but sadly Arush couldn't wish her. On the next working day, Arush eagerly waited for Aditi as he wanted to know Ishika's reaction on his friendship proposal.

"What did she say?" he asked Aditi.

"Who she?" she replied.

"Ishika! You idiot!" Arush said.

"Ohhoo she, she said yes." Aditi said with a smile.

This made Arush's day a successful day. Aditi told Ishika about Arush's wish that he wanted to be her friend and she agreed.

Then Aditi explained him "Ishika is a girl being shy she'll never initiate things. Even if she agreed, you'll have to start a conversation."

"But what will the whole class think? How awkward this will be? How can I suddenly start talking to her?" Arush came out with these questions.

"Dude, are you sick or something?? Do one thing, continue thinking about what others will think and forget about the friendship" Aditi scolded.

"Ok. I'm sorry. I'll talk to her" Arush agreed.

Now things were in favour of Arush as Ishika was referring him for the notebooks for work completion. They started having small conversations. And the best part for Arush was listening his name from Ishika.

He came to know, Ishika was a big fan of Atif Aslam. He then decided to make a list of all the songs of Atif Aslam and give it to Ishika. He made a hand-written list of all his songs and kept it. When Ishika asked for his

English notebook, he kept that list in the notebook. By then Arush tried to know everything about her. Her likes- dislikes, her favourites, her hobbies, her aim, her passion everything. He wanted to know about things that made her happy. He always wished to help her in order to see that amazing smile on her face.

When Ishika returned his notebook, there was a big surprise for Arush. On the last page of the notebook, there was a message for Arush saying "Thank you for everything" with a complimentary close "Shayad your friend." Those words mesmerised him. It was like the dream come true. Finally, the journey of their friendship began after almost 1.5 years of her arrival in the school. Maybe the thankyou was for that list, or for his notebooks, whatever be the reason it made him happy as from then, they were friends, sorry "shayad wale friends!"

Ishika wrote that message with pencil and had asked him to erase it after reading. But for Arush this was the first memory, a very special one of their friendship so he decided to keep it. He tore out the page from his notebook and kept it in his personal dairy.

"Isn't it amazing how small things done by the special one, the person you like or love becomes the biggest achievement of our life."

It was just a thankyou but it was from Ishika. For Arush, it was the first message from her, it was an official confirmation of their friendship, it was much more than what it really seemed to be. It was just the beginning, after that there were many more thankyou and sorry on the last page of his biology, economics, Hindi, English notebooks. He kept every single message in his dairy as the memory of their friendship. This friendship and every little thing done by Ishika was like a beautiful dream for Arush and he wanted to capture every moment in his diary for lifetime. With each passing day, Arush was adding a new chapter of friendship in his life.

Now, it was the time for winter vacations. For other students, they were holidays but for Arush they were 10 days without Ishika. It was difficult for him but he had no choice. Also, just after the vacations it was his birthday on 5th January. But as his friendship with Ishika was just limited to those sorry and thankyou on the notebook so she was not aware of his birthday.

On the other hand, as Ishika was the prettiest girl of the class many boys were trying to impress her. Be it Ishmit or Ashutosh, many wanted to become her "boyfriend". Many of them had her phone number and they used to talk to her on phone and messages. But she never bothered and they all were just good friends to her. Arush often thought, if none of them could impress her then why will she fall for him.

Arush was aware of this truth and had two choices; either he can be sad as he can't be the crucial part of her life or he can be happy by the thought that he has an opportunity to become a small part of her life.

And he decided to be happy by the small things he has got instead of being sad.

It was 5th January, Arush's birthday. It was Sunday so after taking all the calls, replying all the messages from friends and relatives he got ready and went to his friend Rohit's house. He reached there; Rohit wished him and asked him to save his contact number on his phone. Arush was done with saving the number and was waiting for Rohit. He accidently opened the call logs and found a call from "ISHU", which was Ishika's nickname. This left Arush was surprised. The very first thought that popped into his mind was take her number. But then it was a wrong way to take the phone number of any girl without her permission. He kept his decency aside and memorized her number. He thought this might be god's secret gift for him on his birthday. This gift made his day.

Chapter 7

Step In The World Of Competition

Now, Arush had her number, but Arush did't had any personal mobile phone but at that time fortunately Arush's uncle was out of town and he had left a temporary phone for Arush. So It was difficult for Arush to resist himself from texting Ishika and finally he texted her a friendship text. Quickly he got the reply 'who is dis...?" from Ishika. Arush smartly replied to her text "sorry that message was text to you by mistake, wrong number, Arush". Even though he texted her intentionally but to maintain his decency he had mentioned that it was send by mistake & mentioned his name also just to let her know that its Arush. She replied "is this really Arush..?", and then Arush made his confirmation that it was really himself. That's how their first conversation on text started.

Ishika didn't seem much interested in talking to Arush, so Arush didn't text her further. After 4 days, there was an entrance test of reputed coaching institute of city for JEE. That was for the first time when Arush listened about JEE, but he was still appearing in the entrance test just because of Ishika and some of Arush's friends were appearing in it. Since Ishika had prepared for this entrance exam so on the day of exam Arush texted her "All the best'. She replied "thanks & same to you'. Entrance exams was over, as Arush was not at all serious for it so it was the casual one for him. But for many of his friends including Ishika, it was very important, they worked hard for it.

After a week, it was the time for the results of entrance exam, Arush got 159th rank, Ishika 129th, Ashutosh 131st. but the most surprising one was of Sameer, he ranked 15th, that was just amazing. Now Arush was disappointed with himself and he was feeling regret that if he too had taken the exam seriously then there was the chance that he too can get better rank but unfortunately he hadn't. And Arush thought that if had ranked better then there was definitely a chance for him to come in a eye of Ishika. And now it was Sameer who was in the lime light and he really deserve to be. And even Ishika was praising for Sameer's brilliant performance, that was somehow making Arush feel jealous.

Now Arush was feeling bad with this result, he felt small as he thought his goals were small. He was just looking for the better results of boards whereas his friends from now onwards preparing for JEE.

"It's a great saying that to achieve big, you have to dream big, then only you can achieve something big in your life, but if your goals will be small then the achievement will also going to be small"

Now new worries were emerged in Arush's life, and those worries were related to career because Arush had not yet decided that what he wanted to do in his life, but this entrance exam forced him to think about JEE. So Arush decided that he will continue higher studies with science stream & will prepare for JEE. The reason behind this was not only that entrance exam but; main reason was Ishika, as she was too going take the same stream & will prepare for JEE and Arush was planning to do some brilliant work in this field with his studies so that he can impress Ishika.

Now the problem in front of Arush was that 'how to prepare for JEE..? As JEE is considered to be one of the toughest entrance exams in India, and to crack it, one should needed to be highly determined, hardworking, work proper time management under proper guidance. For all these things Arush needed to join coaching institute for JEE but these institution cost an expensive fees and since Arush belonged to a middle class family so joining an expensive institute just for coaching will definitely disturb financial balance of Arush's family and Arush was aware about all these things so he decided to drop the plan of joining the institute for coaching.

Now the challenge for Arush was that how to prepare for JEE, all these things had disturbed him completely, all the time he just used to thought about coaching, preparation and all and that turned him to be complete silent person. He used to remain silent most of the time and his silence was quite surprising for the whole class, as Arush was considered to be one of the talkative students of the class who often used to trouble teachers with his doubts which automatically entertain the whole class. So everyone was concerned about Arush and they want to know the reason behind the silence of him.

Arush had reasons, one was related to his studies apart from that there was another reason and that was, there were rumours in the class that one of their senior from class 12th named Aditya proposed Ishika and she said yes to him. Even though that was rumour but somehow Arush believed that it's true, that had disturbed him completely.

As Arush silence was noticeable to the whole class and this time it was even noticed by Ishika too. So she texted Arush "how was you..?"

Arush replied "fine".

"really?" she said.

"yep" Arush replied.

Then Ishika asked him reason behind his silence. Arush felt happy that atleast Ishika noticed him she was concerned about his happiness. Initially He didn't tell her but when she forced him then he told her that he was upset because of his studies and he was also not able to join the coaching institute. After knowing the complete truth, Ishika was very much impressed with the thoughts of Arush that he was so mature & concerned about the financial condition of his family. So she messaged Arush "you are really a true legend Arush".

Now Ishika was having a great sense of respect for Arush and they were having regular chats through text messages. Ishika often used to say Arush that he is really a great person and going to be very successful in his life. Ishika had belief on Arush's abilities even more than Arush. But Ishika was yet not aware about the one more reason behind Arush's upsetness, that was Aditya's proposal for Ishika.

Arush was happy that then he had turned to be a good friend of Ishika, but those rumours were still hurting Arush so he still used to remain silent in the class. One day Ishika came in front of the seat of Arush, she put a chair their so that she sit there and talk to Arush. She sat there and then asked Arush that "what's the problem..?", can't you be happy..!!! Her tone was soft & sweet and there was a kind of concern in her tone for Arush. She was just trying to say Arush to be happy. At the moment there was no limit of Arush's happiness, he was very happy that Ishika was so much concerned for his happiness. Arush find himself at the top of the world because the Ishika Malhotra, the diva of the school, the girl whom he loves was sitting in front of him just to swing his mood.

"HAPPINESS: Sometimes thousands of efforts are not enough to bring happiness in once life & sometimes a small concern of a special person for you brings it all in a moment. That's the power of love"

Chapter 8

A Step Closer To Their Freindship

Now Arush & Ishika were good friends, they used to share their problems with each other. One day, Ishika messaged Arush that she wants the biology notebook of Arush, but then there was 3 days of school holiday at that time. When he saw that message he immediately replied "how, I mean when & where you will take my notebook..?" but didn't get any reply. Then Arush decided to give the notebook to Aditi as she was the neighbour of Ishika. Arush went to Aditi's home and gave her the notebook & asked her to give it to Ishika.

Arush again messaged Ishika just to tell her that she can take notebook from Aditi. But again she didn't respond, now Arush was getting worried that why Ishika was not replying for his messages. Was she got hurt by any of the action of Arush unwillingly..? Arush send lots of sorry to Ishika. But didn't get any response. Arush tried so many times but didn't get ay reply and then he finally gave up and realized that this was the weird ending of their friendship.

Now school got reopened after 3 days Arush was afraid about Ishika's reaction, so he was just trying not to make an eye contact with Ishika because he was in great guilt that he had hurt Ishika. But that was just the assumption of him.

During lunch break Ishika came to talk Arush with her friend and said "Arush I had kept something in your bag, so please take care that no one else should see it other than you." Arush replied "ok.." Now Arush heartbeats were getting faster, he was just thinking that what Ishika had kept in his bag, but unfortunately he was not supposed to see it in school as Ishika had already warned him not let anyone else to see that.

As Arush reached his home, he immediately looked inside his bag, there was letter, and some chocolates, Arush opened the letter, the letter was full of sorry & thank you. As Ishika was feeling sorry for not replying from 3 days even though Arush helped her and she had mentioned the reason for not replying with this, Ishika added some more happiness in the life of Arush.

Arush added those letter in his file where he kept the all the thankyou and sorry notes of Ishika and that's how with the passing time they were getting closed to each other. They usually use to ask each other about their likes & dislikes and finally one day Ishika asked Arush about his first crush. Arush was always afraid to confess his feelings to Ishika because he just didn't want to lose Ishika and her friendship. But, when Ishika forced her then finally Arush told her that Ishika itself was his first crush. Ishika was surprised to know that but it didn't affect their friendship.

Now it was February, last month to be together for the class as in march there will be board exams then the class will be going to scatter in different atreams. So there were no regular classes, whole class used to bunk and play games. But in all these Arush still seems to be silent sometimes because rumours related Aditya & Ishika were still troubling Arush. One day, when whole class was playing some game, Arush smiled eventually and Ishika immediately caught him and said "chalo finally kisi ke chehre pe hasi to aayi' and whole class got that Ishika was referring to Arush with that. Till that time it was known to whole class that Arush like Ishika. Till last week of February they had some other memorable moments with class, then there were the board exams and after that a 2 month vacation which means 2 months for Arush without seeing Ishika.

Actually, Arush & Ishika were just good friends, but Arush made another imaginary world of himself and Ishika where he had kept all the memories related to Ishika and her friendship till date. For everyone, Ishika was one of the most beautiful and fancy girl but for Arush, she meant to his world where her general concern for Arush makes him happy and any kind of rumour that relates her with any other makes him sad, that was strange but true.

Chapter 9

A Ride To Be Remembered Forever

Now board exams were over and two months vacation was going on, Arush had not seen Ishika since from last one and months. But they used to talk on messages, as Ishika now got to know that Arush likes her, so she clarified Arush that there was nothing between Aditya and Ishika. She cleared it not because she was too interested in Arush but because she just didn't want Arush to be sad because of her, as being her friend she really cares for Arush.

One day there was the call from school. Arush and all his classmates had to report in the school for some official work, Arush informed Ishika about this, requested her to report with Arush so that they can meet after so long time, but unfortunately their timing mismatched and Arush missed the chance to meet Ishika in the school. Since Arush was not able to meet her so in a hope to see Ishika he decided to go to meet Rohit as Rohit & Aditi were the neighbours of Ishika so there was the chance for Arush to see Ishika.

Arush was on his way to Rohit's home and he find a pretty and attractive girl in black dress, she was pretty and seems to be Ishika so Arush slowed down his scooty just to see that girl, and that was Ishika. A pretty and beautiful girl for Arush, who else it can be other than Ishika. Arush beholded her beautiful face, then went to Rohit's home, but he was still wishing to see her once again, so he quickly turned his scooty, crossed her once again, this time he asked her casually that does she want a lift..?

Arush never expected that Ishika will take a lift from him but she surprised Arush by saying yes, and she was angry with Arush that he didn't asked her for the lift when he passed her earlier. That was like dream come true for Arush, love of his life, the most beautiful girl of their school, the Ishika Malhotra was on his back seat. It was a very short ride hardly for 5 minutes but in those 5 minutes Arush had lived his unforgettable dream life. And that added some more beautiful memories in the bond of Arush & Ishika.

That was the first time when Ishika find Arush smart, as she didn't expected that he can look so good, she thought Arush can only look studious in any manner. Arush had brought some chocolates for Ishika and when he dropped her near her home, he gave him those chocolates and that's how another precious moment for Arush ended.

Now it was the time for the results of 10th board, and Arush hardwork proved his abilities. He got it on "bulls eye". Because he scored CGPA 10, that was the great achievement, firstly he shared this news with his uncle, who had major role in each every success of Arush as he was the one who given him such a great upbringing from his childhood. Then after he informed the good news to his parents, and then finally he called Ishika, but she didn't picked it. So he texted her about his result, she didn't replied.

He got the reply on facebook from the elder sister of Ishika, Aashi, she was tall, pretty, stunning and beautiful same as Ishika. Apart from that, she was most important in the life of Ishika, she was not her sister, but she was the support system of Ishika, she was simply meant to be her life. She knew Arush and she even knew that Arush like Ishika. Aashi congratulated Arush for his result, and then Arush asked her about Ishika, she said "Ishika was not happy with her result and bit a upset so she will talk to you later".

In the evening Ishika congratulated Arush and said that she was really happy for Arush but bit a upset to because of her own result, then Arush consoled her. Arush got brilliant results but this was not the end, there was a long journey ahead and now his next goal was JEE, since Arush was not going to any coaching institute so he knew getting a admission in IIT was next to impossible for him, but if he will work hard then he can definitely manage to get a reputed government engineering college.

Chapter 10

Lunch Box....!!

Now they were moved on to class 11th, class was scattered a bit because different student had chosen a different stream. But the good news for Arush was that Arush & Ishika were in same class moreover now Ashutosh was no more the part of their class, he was in another section as he had chosen some other additional subjects. But this doesn't mean that there will be no more troubles in the love story of Arush. As story without a villain never sounds good. So there were some other villains in the story of Arush as well.

At the starting, it was going good, there were no such happenings that can hurt Arush, they had some new faces in the class and one of them was Vikas, who used to sit with Arush. Arush often used to look Ishika and when she caught him that he was looking at her, she wiggle her eyes in order to Arush "what happen,,?'' & Arush replied with a smile "nothing". That's how they had a non verbal conversation in the class. And since Vikas used to sit with Arush so he noticed this non verbal conversation between Arush & Ishika. And one day he finally asked Arush that what was going on between Arush & Ishika. Arush told him everything about his feelings for Ishika.

Arush & Ishika used to talk regularly through messages, they daily decide not to talk for more than 5 minutes, as now it was crucial for time for both of them and they both need to focus on their studies. But their conversation never ends in 5 mnutes and it often turned to continue for hours. This shows that with passing time their bond of friendship was getting stronger.

These conversations with Ishika let Arush to know more about her, and he got to know the importance her elder sister Aashi in the life of Ishika. The nick name of Ishika was Ishu, and other than studies Ishika used most of the household works such as cooking, cleaning etc in the absence of her mother and she even help her mother in cooking & cleaning when her Aashi di got engaged with her college work. And one funnier thing about Ishika was that Arush got to know that Ishika loves to sleep all the time.

After knowing all these things about Ishika, Arush now had more respect & love for Ishika in his heart. He felt proud of Ishika that the girl who so extra ordinary that she manages so many things all together apart from studies. She was really an ideal girl, a caring daughter, a loving sister, a naughty friend and a brilliant student. She was playing all the roles in her life perfectly. Apart from that she was a very nice person, simple, sweet and mature girl.

One day Arush & ishika were discussing about her cooking, so just for fun Arush said to Ishika that he want to eat something cooked by Ishika.

"really...!! " she replied.

"yes...!!" Arush said.

"Ok" she replied.

Next day, after the morning assembly, when Arush was just checking his bag for the notebook he found a unknown tiffin in his bag. Arush thought it was someone else tiffin and someone put it in his bag by mistake. Arush went in front of the class and made the announcement of that unknown tiffin so that the real owner of the tiffin can take the tiffin back. After making the announcement Arush got a response in sweet voice "it's mine" from Ishika. Arush was surprised that how had ishika's tiffin reached in his bag. After some time Ishika passed him a letter and there was message for Arush in that "budhu, vo tiffin mera hai, and main tumhare liye layi hu, kl humari bat hui thi na....." that was wriiten on that letter. After reading this again there were no limits of Arush's happiness and he realized that he was definitely a special one for Ishika. He kept that letter in his pocket and opened the tiffin, as Ishika had yet not taken it back from Arush. There was poha in that which was very delicious & tasty.

After that day Arush getting the vibes that "Ishika might have a same feeling for him as Arush feel for her that's why she like to talk to him and even bought a tiffin for him made by her".

That was the point from where things can be changed because of such thoughts of Arush. As Ishika never had that kind of feeling for Arush, Arush was definitely her very special friend, she cares for him, she respects him, even she likes him but as a friend. All that special things she do for Arush just for his happiness, because she knew that even a small effort from the person whom we love or like meant very special. So she was just trying to give the part of happiness to Arush with her genuine efforts because she thought Arush really deserves to be happy.

Ishika was very much thoughtful, and concerned for Arush was really lucky that she got a friend like Ishika. But Arush's thoughts were leading him to somewhere else, now he was having a sense of expectation in his mind. And expectation is something that turns a happy man to be sad because if once we start expecting in any relation, then we will start going to hurt ourselves too. Same can be happen with Arush as till now he was living his life in a hope that's why even a small effort of Ishika makes him happy but now he was living with expectation.

———◆———

"Allow you to be happy in any circumstances & situations, but expectations always let you to demand for such situations & circumstances that makes you happy", so always be hopeful but never have expectations in your life...!!!

Chapter 11

Love Of My Life...!!!

Now there was the event of youth parliament in the school in where teams from different schools will participate. Arush & Ishika were too the part of it from their school team. Arush was happy with this because now he will get one hour to spend with Ishika, as their whole class will not going to be there during the rehearsals, so Arush can enjoy that one hour of rehearsal with Ishika.

Well it was not that easy to have quality time with the most beautiful girl of the school, as if you want to achieve something big, then you have to face difficulties of that level too and same case was about having a quality time with Ishika, it was difficult to find her alone as she always used to be her with friends, no boy ever missed the chance to flirt with Ishika.

As boys never miss the chance to flirt with Ishika, one of them was shekhar, he was the classmate of Arush & Ishika, he usually used to flirt with Ishika and he was too part of their team and that was the barrier for Arush that was allowing him to talk to Ishika. Shekhar always used to sit beside Ishika during rehearsals and that was intolerable for Arush and even hurting him too because he expected that Ishika will sit beside him by herself during rehearsals.

Now there was a transformation in the mind of Arush, until he didn't expected anything from Ishika, even her single look was the part of happiness for him, at that point he never bothered with whom she was with or she was talking to any other boy or not. For Arush those simple thank you & sorry wriiten on the last pages of the notebooks of Arush by Ishika were part of happiness for him. But now when he started expecting, even though Ishika was sitting in front of Arush instead of being happy he was upset because she was sitting with Shekhar and having fun.

Now there were just 4 days left for the competition, all the team members were called for the rehearsals on the school holiday, on 9th August, it was the event of Eid. That was a rainy day so most of them were reached late, when Arush reached school he didn't find Ishika there, so he was waiting for her, as Arush was there only for Ishika, he was not playing a important role so his presence or absence doesn't make any difference in the rehearsals. It was still raining, most of the team members were yet not came, Arush's hopes were getting down as he thought Ishika will not come. Even the best friend of Ishika, Ayesha was not going to come because of Eid.

There were fewer possibilities that Ishika will come and that had made Arush sad. But suddenly a miracle happen, a girl with wet hairs which were flopped all over her face and then she tucked her hair behind her ear and she was the beauty ''The Ishika Malhotra''.

Ishika wasn't too conscious about her looks, never had a makeup and some strands of her hair were often were on her forehead. Arush always wish to brush those strands of hairs away from her face. So whenever he saw her so, he gave her a gesticulation about it and then she tucks her hair behind her ears that was something that makes Ishika more attractive.

Now things were on Arush's way as there was no Shekhar in rehearsals to trouble Arush and also no Ayesha so Ishika now will definitely prefer to sit with Arush. The rehearsal didn't go that long most of the team members were not able to come because of rain. Arush enjoyed that day a lot with Ishika, he proposed her so many times on that day. Ishika had bring her phone so she was showing her pictures to Arush. Ishika was looking damn beautiful, admirable, adorable and alluring in those pictures, so Arush asked her for those pictures, at first she said no, but when Arush insisted her then she finally got agreed.

That day was the memorable one Arush as Arush & Ishika had spend that day like married couples and after the rehearsals they walked together till the gate. After that day whole school was aware with the fact that Arush like Ishika. Just before the day of event Arush asked Ishika to have click with him and she agreed.

Now it was the day of event 12th august. Ishika had to wear a saree as being one of the Member of Parliament; she came school in a usual school dress. Arush was excited to see her in saree and finally the most awaited moment for Arush had came, Arush had seen her in saree and she was looking gorgeous in the saree. Arush really find himself ugly in front of her at that moment. Arush too need to change his dress as being a press member he need a wear a suit. Just before the performance of their team, Ishika called Arush and said that Arush was not supposed stare Ishika during her performance as according to her if she will have a eye contact with Arush during her performance then she will definitely forget her dialogues.

"Sometimes girls can come up with the simplest of statements, which have most complex meanings".

Her statement had confused Arush what does she really mean, does he influence her that much or she was too having kind of attraction towards him. Such questions raised in the mind of Arush and soon he ignored them without answering. Now it's time for their performance, so Arush wished her a good luck, they had a great shot.

After the performance everyone was busy in changing their get up, even Ishika too, Arush felt sad that she forgot their click, so he thought to just once remind her, so he went to her and asked "what about our click..??", she replied "how is it possible in front of everyone". Arush said "ok" in anger. Ishika quickly got his anger as she was the girl who understands him the best, so she put his hands in her hand and said "chalo, ab itni si baat pr muhh phool jata hai". That was sweet, then he took Sneha with them for taking their picture and finally they had a picture together, Arush was in suit and Ishika was in saree. Both of them were looking like a wedding couple in that photograph.

———————◆———————

Chapter 12

Change is The Only Constant

On 27th august, it was eve of Janamastmi, their usual chats were going on, Arush was wishing from the long time to show his childhood photograph to Ishika so finally he send that photograph to her on that day through multimedia message. After seeing that photograph, Ishika was falling in love with photograph as she found it that much cute. Arush already knew that she will going to like it that's why he was wishing to send it to her, then they started an argument that who was cuter in childhood. Arush was saying Ishika & Ishika was saying Arush. And finally Arush won the argument and Ishika ended by saying "Arush tumse baato main jeetna impossible hai".

Till next week things were normal between them but after that things were changed with between them for no reason. Was that the indication of upcoming storm in the life Arush & Ishika that will going to destroy everything between them or that change was genuine.

Now Ishika started ignoring him, she never replied for his messages, whenever Arush's phone blinks he looks it in a hope that there will be message from Ishika but there was only disappointment for Arush. He passed some sleepless nights in the wait of her message but didn't get any response. He thought that Ishika will definitely clarify him for not responding but she didn't. Arush felt bad and decided to talk to Ishika and ask her the reason behind the change in her behavior. But she avoided to talked to him.

Arush was not able to accept the change in the behavior of Ishika, the girl who always bother to clarify every small to him now not responding for his messages from last few weeks without any reason. Arush requested her so many times to just tell him his mistake but she didn't bother. As Arush still thought she was just punishing him for some mistake.

Finally after long time one day she messaged him "nothing had happened, I was just busy in studies and my phone less, so from now onwards we will not going to talk regularly". That's all she said and ended. Arush find sense in her message because they really consume too time in their chats in such a crucial years of their life.

Even though, she had already told him the reason behind the change but Arush was still not able to accept the things because now she don't even exchange the usual smile with Arush. And that was troubling Arush. And his troubles were not end here as he got to know that his seat partner Vikas likes Ishika and he was even trying to approach her. He roams around her home; he follows her to her coaching. Vikas was also considered to be a good friend of girls as girls were impressed with his singing so they were too helping him in building her friendship with Ishika, they became friends soon & even exchanged contact numbers.

All these were hurting badly to Arush, as on one side differences between Ishika & Arush were increasing with each passing day and on other side Vikas & Ishika were getting closer. Vikas was trying to impress Ishika with his singing; they used to discuss their whatsapp chats in the class. Ishika used to came to his seat but not to talk to Arush but just to listen the song of Vikas. These things were intolerable for Arush and he was still wondering that why she was doing this with him.

"Is this a part of girl's nature that when they got to know that a particular boy likes her, then the girl will give extra attention to that boy."

From all these things Vikas was now turned to be his enemy and the new villain in the story of Arush. Then, Arush too got to know that Ishika was not talking to him not because it consumes her too much time as her time was still consuming in talking to Vikas and she was equally using her phone too. She just didn't want to talk to Arush that's why she had given a fake reason to Arush for not talking to him.

Now Arush decided that he will never try to talk to her because he thought that his place had been replaced by Vikas in the life of Ishika so it's better to stay away from her. Well, now Arush was staying away from Ishika and at the same time Shekhar, Vikas and some other who liked her trying to get close to her. They used to sit around her & talk to her for hours. Things were hurting Arush but he was not supposed to express his pain as now there was no one to understand his pain, he had lost her.

They were nothing more than strangers now, but Arush still love her or maybe it was his never ending love for Ishika. Arush was having a inferiority complex in his mind, he assumed that being with Ishika was a dream and till now he was just living in that dream. Now that dream had broken so he need get back into reality. Ishika was an angel for him, so it's not a big deal for her to forget Arush.

For next few months they didn't had a single word with each other, in this duration Arush got to know that Ishika was in a relationship with Jatin, a boy from her previous school, he already heard about him from Ashutosh as Ashutosh used to tease Ishika with this name in her starting days of school. And Arush now got bonded to her elder sister Aashi, they used to talk facebook, even though Arush & Ishika were not talking to each other but he still care for her that's why he was in a contact with her sister and often wait for Aashi to come online on facebook.

Aashi was the engineering student. She was in her second year of college. She was sweet towards Arush, even she liked him because she was impressed with his thoughts. As Arush already knew that Ishika will never going to be with her, still he care for and love her because his philosophy on love was "It is not everyone's destiny to get the person whom you love, but to love that person is always in once destiny". His thoughts makes him different from other boys.

Now again Ishika's birthday was coming, they were not talking from last few months, but his priority was only her happiness, he just want t to make a try for her happiness on the occasion of her birthday. So he decided to buy a ribbon wrist watch with 7 ribbons of different colours and a Cadbury celebration. He wrapped the gift with colour paper and on 9th November he secretly put it in her bag, as on 10th November again it was school holiday.

As clock strikes the 12'o clock, he wished to message her but he couldn't because he was not talking to her from last few months and his uncle also didn't allowed him to use the phone because he got know about messages of Arush & Ishika. He got angry on Arush and warned him clearly he was not supposed to talk to her at any condition; it was quite obvious no parents want their children to have love life in school time. So Arush slept that night without wishing her.

Next morning, he went to his friend's home and gave her the birthday wishes through text message from his friend's phone. Now he was eager to know that whether she liked his gift or not so he asked her sister about it and she replied "Ishu liked it".

Then very next day to her birthday, there was the birthday celebration in the class. Arush left the class with his few friends as he didn't want to be the part of it. When he came back, Ishika was having some clicks with friend and they had one picture with the Abhishek of 11th C, after having that click there was uneasiness in eyes of Ishika, she quickly took the phone and deleted that photograph. Arush noticed all this and realized that how concerned she was for her relationship and he decided to never ever affect her relationship because her happiness depends on her relationship and Arush just wanted her to be happy.

———◆———

Chapter 13

Heart is Yet To Be Broken Completely...!!

Well, this academic year had not only let Arush to meet the new enemy like Vikas but also let him to meet some friends for life in form of Arham and Shiv Pratap. Arham was the boy with great sense of humour and really a true friend and Shiv Pratap was the decent boy and was another gift of god for Arush in name of friendship. After the birthday of Ishika, things were remain same between them. But now Arham & Arush usually like to trouble Vikas, as he always try to become oversmart in front of girls, especially in front of Ishika.

The transformations that had taken place in life of Arush had also transformed him, now he turned to be the taunt king, who always talks in the satirical tone, even if he say something normally that too sounds like a satire. But somewhere between these satires that old Arush still exist who was living in a hope that she will come back in his life and everything will be alright one day.

Finally the candle of hope had lightened for a while on his birthday 5th January, she wished him and that was enough for him. Then during lunch break she had put something in the bag of Arush got to know about this when Ashutosh & Shekhar were checking out his for chocolates and they found a well wrapped gift in his bag. Arush was surprised to see that and soon realized that only Ishika can do this, but the problem was that gift was in the naughty hands of Ashutosh and how to get it from Ashutosh without letting him to unwrap it, then the life line of Arush, Arham came and handled the situation smartly by saying that it was gift for Arush from their primary teacher. And finally he got it back.

As soon as he reached the home. He immediately opened it and saw it; there were no limits of his happiness because she gifted him a photo frame with the childhood photos of Arush & Ishiika framed together. That was the best gift he had ever received and with this gift all the quarries between them were ended in a moment. Arush called her, she was waiting for his reaction, so he said thank you to her. Her gift had showered the water on the plant of their friendship.

"Why she had done so,,?, "Does she still care for me..?, "She too don't want to lose me..?" such questions were raising in the mind of Arush, then next to his birthday finally after so long time he went to talk to her. At that time he was really wishing that his birthday should last for a little longer time. They had usual "hi-hello" and then things were as it as they were before because she was engaged in organizing the farewell party for seniors with Ashutosh and Arush just hate it to see her with Ashutosh. As Ashutosh was the person, who troubled and teased her a lot in the starting even he made her cry but she forget everything and working together with him.

Arush was not at all interested in the farewell party, as he didn't want Ishika to be a part of such gatherings, because he didn't want that Ishika's beauty to be displayed in front of everyone. For him, Ishika was very precious so he just wanted to keep her beauty hidden from the eyes of everyone. These were thoughts of Arush. Arush had no plan on going to farewell party but when Aashi insisted him as Aashi means a lot to him so he couldn't deny her.

Now it was the day of party 21st January, Arush knew that Ishika will going to look gorgeous, beautiful and adorable in the party and Ashutosh, Shekhar & Vikas will not going miss the chance to stick with her. That's why Arush was not in a mood to go to party but just because of Aashi he went there. Ishika was looking gorgeous as expected, but as Arush entered the hall he start getting negative vibes that something will happen that will hurt him badly. And it really happened, Ishika was having clicks with other boys, things not end here, she had done a couple dance with Ashutosh, that moment had completely broken Arush and he was no more able to resist the atmosphere of the party so he left the party.

Chapter 14

Beautiful Memories Recreated..!!

Arush was disturbed badly with what had happened in the farewell party, but now exams were near and so he tried to make himself busy in his studies. Exams got over, results came he got 84% and promoted to the final year of the school and the crucial one too.

The year was important for him in many respects as this would be his last year with Ishika and he want to make himself the unforgettable one for her, to be the reason behind her happiness, to turn her each moment into happiness, to turn each and every day of her life special. That was the great Arush, who had been hurt so many because of Ishika and still just wishing her happiness. Apart from that, the year was crucial for him from his career point of view, he had 12th boards and JEE.

There was some good and bad news for Arush at beginning of academic year. Good news was that the so called lover of Ishika, Vikas was no more the part of the class. As he was failed in class 11th so repeating the same class. And the bad news was Arham had to leave the school due to some personal reasons.

Since it was the last year so Arush forgot everything that had happened in the past and tried for the new beginning of their friendship. As:

"Love is like life, where you don't find smooth roads always, where you don't achieve goals so easily, you have to struggle for it but when you don't stop living your life; why should one stop loving someone?"

Finally, he started talking to Ishika at the beginning of academic session and this time with no hesitation in his mind, he was free to speak anything, didn't care about what the whole class will think and this "who cares' attitude had worked for him soon they become good friends as they were efore and Arush realized that she always had a respect for his feelings but she just can't be with him so she don't want to hurt him that's why she was keeping distance with him.

Arush usually used to stand in front of her seat for hours and talk to her and even sometime he sit beside her, during their talks he often used to say her "I love you" and then she wiggle her eyes in anger and say "Arush..!!' and Arush immediately say "Ishika..!!" with love.

They used to discuss about JEE and 12th results, Ishika used to say that Arush will going to excel in results of JEE as well as of 12th. And same thing Arush used to say about Ishika. He often used to speak negative things like he used to say that "She will going forget him and his friendship after school life and she will not even remember the name Arush". Then she interrupted him in anger saying "Arush' and just pause. He just loves to listen his name in her voice because for him, his name sounds better in the voice of Ishika.

Chapter 15

He Was There With Her, When The World Blames Her...!!

This last year of school was full of happenings for them. Some sweet, heart tickling and some bitter happenings were there but it was a part of their friendship, they better knew how to handle it.

"Ups and downs are important in life to keep us going because even a is straight line ECG means that the person dead".

So they had fights between them but it never lead to break of their bond. Arush often used to do stupid things to convince her, to make her happy and those stupid things were like he used to write "all the very best Ms. beautiful" on the desk on which she will going sit in the exam, before her every exam, whenever he find her upset he write "keep smiling" on her desk or inside her notebook, sounds stupid but these things were good enough to bring smile on her face and to vanish her upsetness.

One day when Ishika was absent, that day was quite free, they were not having the regular classes, then Ashutosh, Ishikam and Satyam from 12th B came to their class & joined Shekhar. They were in a mood of making fun of everyone, so one by one they were making fun of everyone, even though no one was listening to them still they continued to do the same. Then they finally came on Ishika, as Ishika was the special one so when everyone came on her suddenly paid attention to them. Then they started speaking rubbish things about Ishika in front of whole class, they were presenting her as a characterless girl in front of everyone.

Arush decided to stop them but he thought it will create more issues so he stopped himself. Because such foolish acts were not at all needed to be responded, those were the boys who once used to roam around Ishika and now when they don't get what want from her so they started insulting her publically by circulating foolish rumours about her. After when they leave Arush immediately went to Vidya, seat partner of Ishika and requested her to not tell Ishika about all this because it would disturb her and hurt her, and Arush didn't want that.

Next morning Ishika was back to school and she was happy. So Arush got the relief and thought she might not knew about yesterday's happening, but during lunch there was a change on her face, her face was frowned. Then after lunch she was not in the class, that made Arush worried, so he went to look for Ishika and he find her talking to Ashutosh, that hurted him badly because Arush was worried for her and she was busy in talking to Ashutosh, the boy who had said so many rubbish things about her in the past day.

She came back to class crying but Arush didn't say her anything as he thought that she needs Ashutosh more than him in her life. Then for next 4-5 days, she turned into complete silence and Arush can feel the pain behind her silence, he can't see her upset but since he was angry with Ishika so he would not going to talk to Ishika but he simply write "keep smiling" on her desk or on any of her notebook, and when she saw it, she started crying. Then finally Arush asked Aashi about her sadness. Aashi told him that Ishika had fight with her boyfriend Jatin because of that foolish act of Ashutosh & his friends. Even Aashi was worried for Ishika because she was not having proper diet, not even talking to anyone in the family. Those 4-5 days of Ishika's silence were difficult for Arush too as she was only in a habit to see her happy.

The things got automatically soughed out between Ishika and Jatin. She got normal after that he didn't talk to Ishika. After a week, Arush & Ishika were alone in the class and then she asked "What happened..?"

"Nothing" Arush replied,

"So why you are not talking to me..?" She asked.

"I think you don't need me anymore, you have Ashutosh with you" he replied with satire.

"Ohho please Arush!" she said with an irritation.

"Then tell me why you cried when you saw that 'keep smiling'..??" he asked.

"Arush when I saw that keep smiling I felt happy that someone cares so much about my happiness and those tears were of happiness. Happiness of having such a great friend who was there when the world blames me" she said.

Arush got huge warmth after listening these words from Ishika. He felt happy to be reason of the 'tears of happiness' of her .After that their bond became stronger. Thereafter they use to be together most of the time, now not even single day passes in which he don't have a word with her and now even some of the teachers had an idea that something was going on between Arush & Ishika.

Arush often used to stand outside the physics & chemistry labs of the school just to see her as they were in different batches because of alphabetical order of roll numbers. So they were not supposed to attend the same lab together. When Ishika had her physics lab, Arush had to be in chemistry lab and vice–versa. Arush used to bunk his lab and stand outside lab in which Ishika was engaged just to see her because he knew this was the year with Ishika that he was passing so he didn't even want to miss a single moment to see her.

———— ◆ ————

Chapter 16

Somethings That Meant To Be Remembered Forever..!!

Now it was the time for friendship day, Arush wished her with chocolates and she kept something in between his notebook, and asked him to look it after reaching home, he immediately checked his notebook and there was very beautiful handmade greeting for friendship day made by Ishika for Arush. Beauty and level of creativity of that greeting was simply beyond the limits and it was just impossible to describe its actual beauty in words.

"It was made with different colour papers. On its front cover, there was beautifully written "HAPPY FRIENDSHIP DAY" then on its very first page there was an amazing sketch in which a non verbal conversation between a boy & girl sitting in the classroom that was signifying the scene of classroom showing conversation between Arush & Ishika in the class. Then after there was a long message written by Ishika for Arush in which she mentioned his importance in her life. What his friendship meant for her and many more thing that were simply making Arush special in her life. That greeting was really something that any girl will not do this much even for her life partner but Ishika had done it for Arush. This shows that how special he turned to be in her life.

Now it's November and her birthday was near, Arush need to plan a gift for her, something very special for her that would make her to remember Arush forever. He reminded himself that Ishia told him that, her friends from her previous school had arranged a farewell party for her and Raj, one of her friend arranged the cake for the party. Arush thought that even after 4 years leaving that school she still remember Raj so he too decided to do something similar as Raj had done so that she will remember Arush also and that will make him alive in her memories forever.

So there was a plan of birthday celebration of Ishika that will be arranged by Arush and since that was the first and last time she was going to celebrate her birthday in the School. As on her previous birthdays there was always a school holiday. So he want to make it very special and memorable one for her and apart from this, he also decided to gift her teddy so he went to mall with Arham and bought a cute teddy. Now he want his gift to be first gift for her on her birthday and for that he took help of Aashi, he asked Aashi to meet him before 2-3 days of her birthday They met and he gave her wrapped teddy and asked her to give Ishika as the clock strikes 12 on her birthday.

Now it's just one day to go for her birthday, so Arush went to bought a black forest cake in the evening with Arham and then he asked Arham to keep it his home till morning and he told him that in the morning, he will take it back. Finally, it was the day of celebration, when god had lost its most beautiful angel as Ishika, it was her 17th birthday. He messaged her at 12 am in night, he wished to call her but he knew that she will be engaged with Jatin.

In the morning, he got ready for school and went to school. At first he dropped her sister, and then he went to Arham's home to pick the cake. He was in hurry and that cause him to met with the small accident that had damaged his scooty and somehow the shape of cake too. It was not really the great beginning of the big day, he thought Ishika will not going to like the cake as its shape has been disturbed due to the accident he just had. Arush reached school with the cake and managed to make it reach into his class without being highlighted to anyone. After reaching the class he kept the cake in the cupboard, Ishika had yet not came so he was waiting for her. When she came, she was looking even prettier and beautiful than usual days. He wished her and told her that there was something for her in the cupboard.

Ishika was happy after seeing the cake. Arush want everything to be happen perfect on that day. Ishika planned to cut the cake during lunch break and Arush thought that her birthday can be more special for her if he will not be present there. So he tried to hide himself from her during lunch but she was too a stubborn girl and she decided to cut the cake in his presence only and then all her friends were looking for Arush in the whole school. And finally they found him and almost half of the lunch time was passed, Arush thought that cake cutting must be done till now but when he reached the class there was the different scene Ishika had yet not cut the cake, because she was waiting for Arush. When he came in the class, she looked at him with an anger & disappointment. Then finally she cut the cake with Arush and after that she told everyone about my gift that was the teddy. Finally he got what he wanted, the happiness on her face and she even said to him "Arush you made my day thank you so much for doing all thesefor me!"

That's how the birthday celebration was done with adding some more beautiful memories in their friendship. And in this celebration, there was role of Arham and Aashi too who had helped Arush in order to make the things perfect and with this their bond had become even more stronger.

———————◆———————

Chapter 17

Some More Heart Tickling Moments..!!

Now they were very good friends and the bond that they were sharing was very special one for both of them but still Arush always seems to be a little pessimistic in everything and often taunt Ishika with his negative thinking & satirical words. Then she often said "tumhe mere alawa or koi nhi jhel sakta Arush..." and sometimes when Arush act to be little naughty towards her then she says "Arush ... tum chahte kya ho...?" he replied "sabke samne bata du...□"" then she says "Arush...!!!" because she knew exactly what he meant at that point. Such conversations between them were the part of heritage of their bond for Arush.

The autumn break was going on but they had their extra classes so had to come school to attend the extra classes, others were coming to attend extra classes but Arush was coming school just for Ishika, to see her. Her father or her sister often used to come to pick her from school. But one day, she was going alone because that day their class was released earlier than the usual timing. Arush didn't want her to go alone because he didn't want any boy to say something wrong or pass any comment on her. So he immediately went Arham's home and from there he called her sister and she didn't pick the call so he messaged her "Ishu is coming alone from school so ask your father to pick her". He always wished that whenever Ishika was not with him, she must be with her father, as he was very protective and conservative so no boy can even look at her when she was with her father and that's what Arush wanted.

And being conservative and overprotective for his daughters, was quite obvious, as a father of 2 such beautiful daughters, he had to be protective because they were their real wealth and very precious for him so he was just protecting their daughters from the world at every stage of life.

"A father is the one, who holds your finger from your childhood & holds it till the end, he is the one who make you learn how to stand and live with the society, he is the one who become your first identity, he is the one who take responsibility of all your mistakes, he supports you at the every stage of your life, he is the one who always sacrifices his needs just to fulfill your wishes, he is the only person in this world who want you to go ahead him and become more successful than him, he can be just simply defined with the word; - "GREAT"….!!!"

After some days, Arham came to school for some work, he went there to meet Arush. Ishika was also present in the class so Arham went to talk to her and then she said to her "Arush is crazy about you, you know, when you were going home alone, he immediately come to my home just to call your sister so that she will come or send your father to pick you"

"yes, I know lucky girl I m." she replied to Arham.

After listening this Arush shouted in satirical tone "Richie rich". With this he meant boyfriend of Ishika. Then she started crying because she was referring Arush and his friendship with her statement, but Arush thought she was referring her boyfriend.

Arush was wrong at this point, maybe he was able understand her friendship or maybe it was because some hurting happenings of past that had his thoughts to be pessimistic which simply not allowing him to accept that good things can happen in his life. Well, whatever was the reason, but outcome was not good because it cause tears in her innocent eyes. Arush felt guilty for the incident and said sorry to her.

Now it was the time for school's annual function and its rehearsals were going on. Girls from the class of Arush were going to perform a group dance in an annual function. Arush didn't want Ishika to perform because of 2 reasons, firstly if she will going to dance then people will whistle and other such similar things and he didn't want this to happen and secondly, if she will perform then she had to be engaged in the rehearsals for last one hour of the school time and in that one hour, he will not able to see her. But Ishika was the part of group dance and that had turned him to be upset.

One day he went to see her during the rehearsals, Ishika caught him and noticed the upsetness on his face, while all other members were dancing, she took his hand

and asked her to sit down beside her. Then she asked him "What happened?"

"Nothing.." Arush replied..!!

"I know you don't want me to participate in a group dance because you don't want people to see me or to pass comment on me. But Arush, it never matters for me, you are my best friend so please be happy if you will be happy then only I will be able to focus on my dance and if I will not focus then that will spoil my performance and I hope you don't want that my performance to be spoiled so please be happy.." She explained him amatively.

Then she also added "You know, since you don't want me to participate, but I have participated, so I met with an accident, so please happily permit me to perform so that there will be no more accidents for me"

Arush smiled and said "ok…"

Ishika was really the best friend, who understands him the best, she even understand her silence. She was so concerned about the happiness, Arush was really lucky to have her as a best friend. She was letting him to experience the best part of his life and was turning his each and every moment into a happy moment. She was not in a love with Arush but the bond they had was very special one. But it was that enough for Arush or he wants something else…?

Expectation for something else that was the point where he hurt himself and it was not Ishika who was hurting him in-fact she was the only reason behind his happiness but it was his expectation that hurt him every time instead of being happy.

Chapter 18

How He Defines His Good Times

It was the time for the birthday of Arush and undoubtedly Ishika was the one who wished him first, she called him at 12 am in night and wished him. He was happy that love of his life was the first one to wish him on his birthday. In the morning, he went to school, usual day passed for him in the school, everyone wished him including Ishika and one special thing that had happened for him on his birthday was that Ishika agreed to roam with him in the whole school. And when bell rings for school off, she asked him to stay in the class for a while and when everyone was gone, she gave him the plastic bag, there was something in that bag .

Arush understood that it was his birthday gift; he opened it on his way to home, because his excitement not letting him to wait anymore and he found a brand new black shirt. Arush was shocked and equally surprised, Arush was a simple boy, away from the fancy life, he had never imagined that someone will going to gift him such an expensive gift. But Arush was now the integral part of the life "The Ishika Malhotra", a fancy girl, who can make any one person's life fancy who was part of her life.

Apart from that there was a beautiful birthday greeting and a small diary in which there were beautiful messages on its each page. After looking all this Arush felt himself at the top of the world as even a small chocolate from the person you love on your birthday can make your day so in their case Ishika had done this much for him and its not only Ishika but Aashi too was involved in this gift because he had special bonding with Aashi too.

Arush too decided to do something special for Ishika that can make her happy. Arush had made a file in which he kept all the sweet and cute things related to their friendship like all her sorry and thank you that she had wriiten on the last pages of his notebook, her suggestions for improvement of handwriting of Arush, the note that she gave him when a brought a lunch for him, their cute fight during the rehcarsals of youth parliament and everything related to her that he had, he put it in that diary, and he had too made a sketch of Ishika, he put that also in that file.

One day he decided to show that file to Ishika so that she will realize that how special she was in his life. Even though she already knew that but Arush once want how she will react after seeing all these. He gave that file to her but the situation was not so that she can see it with Arush so she said to Arush that she will look it at her home. Next day, when she came there was huge smile on her face as she returned that file to Arush, she wants to keep that file with her, but Arush said to her "Ishika you are the most beautiful thing that had happened to my life, so I just want to keep every memory related to you very preciously, because we never know when time will change and whether you will be there in my life or not, but this file memories of our friendship will always with me. That will strength me in my tough time, let me to be happy in situation, so please let me keep this file" these touchy words from Arush really touched Ishika and she smiled and said "ok".

Arush was yet not satisfied with his efforts that he had made for the happiness of Ishika, he was still wishing to do some more for her happiness, some more to make her feel special. This time he tried to do it in a different manner, something with her photographs, and he decided to make a video-slide for her. This idea came in his mind because of Shiv Pratap. Arush saw a video–slide in the phone of Shiv, that one of his friends made for him, and that's how the thought of video slide came in his mind.

He had done this with the help of Shiv, he collected all her pictures, her family pictures, some of her special pictures, pictures from all her notes he had kept in his file including the birthday greetings and friendship day greetings, pictures of that photoframe that she had gifted him and the entry of Ishika in his slam book. And that was Shiv, who arranged all these pictures in a video in manner to make the video perfect. He gave the final touch to the video and put some captions in the video to show how lucky they all were who were part of the life of Ishika. The background song in the video was "jaise tera main... waise mera tu..." when it was completed, it was just amazing and Ishika was very happy with that video.

Ishika had chaged his life completely; she changed the definition of good time for him. "He was with her, that's how he defined his good time". They were in a last few weeks of the school, they had a wonderful year with so many beautiful memories which was going to last forever and now it was the time for their official end of school that was the farewell party. It was on 21st February, the day of happiness and joy for everyone but not for Arush, he was suffering from nostalgic feeling that day, a feeling of sadness because those were the last moments with Ishika for him. After that, they never know whether they will get the chance to have time together or not. These 4 years with Ishika for Arush passed so quickly. It had turned him to be sensitive for Ishika.

Farewell was not the entertaining one for Arush because he was going through so many thoughts in his mind, he was thinking that "Is this time was enough..?", "Do I had done enough for Ishu, so that she will remember me...!!", Had I done enough to be alive in her memory..?" All these questions were raising in his mind and that's how he passed his farewell party.

But actually he had packed so many beautiful memories of those 4 years with togetherness of Ishika in his bags, which were enough to make him happy for his whole life.

Finally Arush convinced himself that now he will be no more connected to her because he knew about his sensitive nature so any contact with her will only going to hurt him more in the future. That was the first time when he sounds to be mature in case of Ishika. He didn't message her for a week but all the time Ishika was there in his mind, like when he thought of cooking, it remind him of tiffin. With tiffin, it reminds him that incident where Ishika brought tiffin for him and then her thought rest on Ishika.

"Isn't it amazing how minds relate one thought from another and finally reached to where it really want to be?"

Arush often thought that may be Ishika was too suffering from the same feeling from which he was going through, because they both were friends, so break in the bond will affect both of them. But soon, he realized that she was a special, there were so many people who like her as Arush do, so why will she miss him.

One day his phone blinked, there was a long message from Ishika with full of frustration and anger, in which she mentioned, that how much she was suffered in this past week, how she missed him, every time he expected a message from him whenever her phone blinks but at the end just got disappointed. This message from Ishika made him happy, he was glad to know that Ishika was too going through the same feeling as Arush was feeling for her in these days. Then he explained her reason for messaging her and finally he conciliated her, then they exchanged the best wishes for boards.

Now both of them were engaged in their studies, there was one important day for both of them in the middle and that was the birthday of Aashi, who was very important person for both of them, it was on 7th march. Arush decided to give her a photoframe with framed picture of Ishika & Aashi and gifted her, this time he took help of Ishika.

———————• ◆ •———————

Chapter 19

Results

Examinations were over now and they were not gone passed as that good for both of them, then they had JEE. That was also not good for both of them. Days were passing usually, they had not seen each other from 2-3 weeks, Arush was missing her, so he put his status on whatsapp "Ishu missing you". But when Jatin, boyfriend of Ishika got to know about this, he got angry and that was quite obvious, no boyfriend would like to see the name of his girlfriend on status on any other boy. He asked Arush to change his status that caused a clash of words between them.

When Arush asked Ishika about this, she said "Jatin is right at this point, Arush just once try to look up the things from his perception, your status was the hurting one from him, so please change it." Ishika was absolutely right because the mistake was of Arush only at this point, but Arush was not able to understand the things because of his obsession for her, he thought that Ishika didn't even bother how he was wishing her and simply asked him to change his status." Arush got hurted, but the mistake was of Arush's only.

Ishika was often troubled and trapped when she got stuck in a situation where she had to make the choice of right and wrong between Arush & Jatin. She was distraught with all such stuffs but still she always handled the situation very maturely, she tried not to hurt anyone, and just expected them to understand her. Ishika was the mature girl, was good enough to judge the things between Arush and Jatin, sometimes she supports Arush too, and fights with Jatin for Arush. Jatin was a short tempered person so she often asked him to be calm like Arush.

But this issue of status had cause a communication gap between Arush & and Ishika. Even though it was the fault of Ishika, but Arush thought that she can't understand his feelings so it's better not to talk to her. On the other hand, Ishika was frustrated with her, with these stuffs related to Arush & Jatin. She want her life to be simple, but it was not that simple as she had thought about her every small action that what will be affected of her action on Arush and Jatin and that doesn't mean that she was interested in both of them. It was just that she cares for both of them as one was her best friend and other was her boyfriend so she just didn't want lose any of them.

The communication gap cause Arush to miss her again, but this time she made herself busy with new friends because she want her life to be stress free. Arush messaged her but she didn't bother to reply; now she was just avoiding Arush, and he was still trying to talk to her even though she never replied for his messages. Arush realized that how much he troubled Ishika when she understood him the most. He always tried to talk to her in a hope that one day she will respond him properly and he will get his Ishu back in his life. But she remain non responsive.

Arush tried to make himself busy in the work of his home and shop. He thought to help his uncle by looking after his shop after all he had done this much for Arush. He looked for the needs and wishes of each and every member of the family without any expectations so Arush just to support his uncle as much as possible by devoting his complete time in shop. His days were turned to a very busy one. And still, his exhausted fingers never forget to type message for her after every hectic day,... but every night his tired eyes fall asleep without getting her reply....!!

Differences between Ishika & Arush were increasing with each passing day, and at the same time social account of Ishika was hacked. Someone misused her account and circumstances let her think that it was done by Arush because he was the one who knows her so well. Arush was not the one but situation and people around Ishika convinced her that it was Arush only. That turned the things even worst between them. She lost the trust on him.

Now there was tension about college, they both were worried whether they will got a reputed engineering college or not, because their result was not good enough. Counseling process was going on, they were done with registration and choice filling was done and it was the time for results of first counseling and it came on 11th July. Ishika called him so many times and finally he picked her call on 8th attempt because he was busy in some work. As he received the call she shouted on him and asked him for his JEE roll no. Even though she shouted on him but there was belongingness in that and Arush was happy with that. She scolded him for incorrect choice filling that cause him to get an ordinary private college and she also informed him that she got chemical branch in one of the reputed government college of state and she was very happy that finally she will be away from the people who had made her life so frustrated. She was happy that now she will her life in her own way.

With this news Arush got a mixed feeling of happiness & sadness. He was happy for the happiness of Ishika and he was sad that now she will go in a different city, away from him, whether they will meet again or not and Arush was yet satisfied with his efforts and he wished to do something very special for her before she was leaving the city.

Arush was just thinking that what to gift her. Then a thought came in his mind that Ishika was going in another city, there she will be away from her family, she had to deal with all the situations alone whether it will be good or bad, so she will definitely miss her family. So he decided to gift her something that will keep her family closed to her even though they were away from her. He gifted her photo frame with multiple photos of Ishika framed in it, each member of her family. He thought that gift will always keep her family close to her, always provide strength to her to deal with the any kind of situation, and it will never let her to be alone.

Arush was very much thoughtful for her and he was just hoping that now she will atleast remember that there was someone in her life named "Arush".

Happiness

"Happiness are any expensive gifts and parties, it is not even in fancy celebration…!!

But actually happiness is when she got a lunch for you by her own.

Happiness is when she strictly interrupt you in an argument.

Happiness is when she clarifies you for having a conversation with any other boy.

Happiness is when she try to conciliate you for her mistake.

Happiness is when you for her credit for her first wish.

Hjappiness is when she continuously talk to you hours without letting you to speak a single word.

Happiness is being with her when she needs you the most.

Happiness is to be the reason behind her smile.

Happiness is listening your name in her voice.

Happiness is what she give, not what you take.

Happiness is something which we usually try to find in the big things but it is actually hidden in a cute heart tickling things…!!!"

———◆———

Chapter 20

Its Destiny...... Believe It Or Not....!!!

Arush tried for the second counseling, this time with proper choice filling, after 15 days result came and it was unbelievable! He thought that things were now over with Ishika but destiny had planned something else for them because he got the same branch and same college as that of Ishika. Arush was happy at the moment and he accepted it as destiny wants them to be together for another 4 years and some more beautiful memories to their friendship. But the second thought came in his mind about Ishika's behaviour in past few weeks towards him. He reminded himself that how she was thinking while she was going away from all those peoples who had made her life so frustrated and Arush was one of them. And he will let her that he too got the same college and branch that will definitely spoil her happiness. So he decided not to tell her about the actual result of counseling. And when she asked him about the result, he said he managed to get a government engineering college but didn't mention the city. She was happy with that and then she added that one of their common friend Arnab too got same college as that of

Ishika but a different, she was very happy to have Arnab there to give her a company.

But the incomplete truth of Arush didn't survive that longer and she got to   know that Arush was too got same college and branch as that of Ishika, which was shocking for her. She was very much upset that destiny had again put them together. All those things from which she want to run away they were now back on her way. Arush felt bad with such reactions of Ishika.

After few days she clearly warned him that they will no more friends in the college, so he must not try to talk to her there. Arush agreed for this just for her happiness.

Arush was already upset with way Ishika responded him and apart from that, there were some other problems waiting for her in his life; his admission was yet not done, his family was not in a favour to admit him in a college which he got in the counseling because they really didn't the importance of government college as there was no one in his family from the engineering background. But Arush knew that somehow he managed to convince his family and finally done with his admission process in new city and new environment.

In the very early days of his college he got knew that his family had a doubt on him that he moved on to new city for college just for the girl that had broken him very badly. He was hurted because he was the brilliant student from starting & never compromised with his studies still his family doubted on him when he was staying away from his family just for his studies. He was really alone at that time, that was the time he needed his best friend Ishika to hold him but the sad part was she was not there for him.

———◆———

Chapter 21

Beginning of College

Their classes were started; he had new friends in the college. He was waiting for the arrival of Ishika, even though they were not going to talk to each other. But still his eyes were looking for her and he waited for her for a week. She didn't come but a news came that she had changed his branch in the internal sliding, and now she was the I.P. branch of the same college. Arush was a bit upset with this news, but then simply he accepted it.

They usually see each other in the college but behave as like they were strangers for each other. They used to ignore each other, didn't even say a casual hi-hello to each other and didn't even exchange the smile. Two months passed in the college they didn't even had a single word with each other. It was really hurting for him and he often thought that was his friendship so ordinary that she forgot everything so easily? As days passed, with each passing day something happens that hurted him. Whenever he heard something about Ishika, whenever he saw her interacting with any other boy, it always hurted him and sometimes he even cried when he felt completely broken.

Now it was a day of an event in the college, they both were the participants of event and it was officially college off day so there was not much rush in the college and then classmates of Arush wished to meet Ishika so he just tried to talk to her and and asked her "my friends were wishing to meet you so can you please fulfill their this wish". And she agreed. That was the first time after almost two and half months they were meeting in the college campus. He was happy with that. Then he took her to his friends and introduced her to the group and they were just having the words with each other. Suddenly one of the friend of Arush asked her "Arush is going to upgrade his branch to I.P., so you will be happy with that...?" she replied "No way, now no more, I had tolerated him enough in 4 years and now, I just want to stay away from him and if his branch got changed then I will apply for college upgrading and will change the college". She said this in a humourous manner but indirectly she simply rejected him in front of his friends. His friends knew about his feelings and they too felt bad the way Ishika insulted the feelings of Arush.

———— ◆ ————

Chapter 22

Birthdays Turning Around The Things...!!

Now her birthday was near, things were not going good in their friendship, but, still Arush collected money through his pocket for her gift and bought 2 salwar suits for her. He was not supposed to give her the gift directly because she didn't want to talk to him so he took help of Aashi for making his gift to be reached to Ishika.

During her birthday, there were Diwali vacations of college and 8th November was the last working day of the college before her birthday. Arush was wishing to meet her once and give her advance wishes, so he requested her to meet him and finally she agreed after making so many excuses and said that she will text or call him at 1pm. he waited till 2 pm but didn't call or message him. Just to remind her about their meeting, finally he called her when he saw her walking ideally with her friends. When she received the call, she didn't even remember about their meeting but she asked Arush wait in the canteen and said that she will be there in 15 minutes. He waited for 30 minutes but she didn't come and again when he called her. She said "Sorry, we can't meet, I'm busy with my friends".

And in this way, she put down all his excitements about their meeting. Arush thought that they will have a small pre celebration of her birthday in the canteen but she disappointed and hurted him very badly because she doesn't care for his feelings and happiness anymore. At that moment tears were automatically rolled out from his eyes. He washed his face so that no one can see him crying. He had some chocolates for Ishika because he didn't want wish her empty handed. He went to Ishika to give her advance wihes and chocolates and went off. And then he decided that not to approach her anymore in near future.

On 10th November, it's her birthday, he decided not to wish her because he thought that he and his wishes no more matters for her so his wishes will only going to spoil her birthday. But he called Aashi just to know that whether Ishika liked her gift or not, but it was Ishika who received the call, he wished her and quickly cut the call.

After that he didn't message or call her for next 2 months. And even learned to ignore her and this kind of attitude turned situation into his favour because now Ishika tried to talk to him. But this time he kept control on his feelings even though he too wanted to talk to Ishika but still avoided to talk to her. He always felt happy whenever he find her message in his phone but never reply until it was not something important. He never keep her chats, as her chat will show her profile picture and her picture was enough to bring the flashback of the beautiful memories of their friendship and that was only going to make him weak and he just didn't want to be that.

One day Ishika messaged him, that was a dare message in which Arush had to dedicate a song to her and when he forwarded it back to her, her dare was to tell 2 things about Arush that she don't like. She replied "firstly your too much negative thinking and secondly, you acts are seems to be fake". Arush didn't got the second one so he asked her about the explanation of it then she explained that from last few months, what Arush was pretending to do, she knew it was fake. He was pretending to be arrogant towards her but she knows the truth that he still feels same for her. Arush was touched with her such words and felt glad with the thought that she still understands his silence and pain behind his words and that's how Ishika proved that she was same girl who once understand the Arush best.

The behaviour of Arush was still same towards Ishika and now it's his birthday and he wanted to be alone on his birthday so he didn't go to his home even though vacations were started. He was alone as the clock strikes at 12, there was a call for him but this it was not Ishika, it was one of his college friend Anand who was the first one to wish him after that it was Ishika & Aashi then there were some more wishes after that the day passed quite normally for Arush and he didn't want it to be special because the only definition of special for him was Ishika and she was no more there in his life.

Arush reached home after his birthday and then Ishika often asked him to meet but he always ignored her because he was just responding her in a same, way as she used to do whenever Arush asked her to meet in the college. But then finally when Aashi asked her to meet he agreed to meet at top n town.

Arush reached there on time then Aashi & Ishika came, both of them were looking gorgeous and beautiful but Arush attention was grabbed by Ishika only as always then Aashi and Arush were talking to each other as they were meeting after long time. Aashi find some changes in the looks of Arush so she told him about that then he ordered some snacks for them as it was his birthday treat then there was the surprise moment for Arush. When Ishika came with a brand new wrist watch and then she gave it to him. There were no limits of his happiness and it was just because of the wrist watch but actually it was because Ishika had done it for him. And if they were not in a public place then definitely Arush had hugged her. He thanked both of them for the gift.

Ishika again proved that she still cares for Arush, still respects his feelings. She was just bounded in the college that's why she was not able to meet him. Her gift had broken his so called attitude that he was retaining from previous 2-3 months. His heart again got melted and fall for her and that's how the great day ended for him.

————— ◆ —————

Chapter 23

Something Special For Aashi Too..!!

They were having the normal conversation now and with these conversations he got to know that Ishika was now turned to be a poet and the best thing about her poetry was that she write to express herself not to impress others. And she also had some good friends in her branch and her best friend was Avika with whom she liked to be most of the time.

When they were coming back after vacations, they were on same train and after half way Arush joined Ishika. "It is always great to have a journey with the person whom you love". But that was not the great one for Arush as Ishika was engaged in her phone most of the time. She was not talking to him. He realized that he was her friend but not as that important as he was before.

They were talking to each other on calls and messages. Sometimes, they even met each other in the college. They talk for hours on call, and they even had a fight but that was a sweet one. She often used to make him listen her awesome poems.

The birthday of Aashi was coming. And Aashi had a crucial role in life of Arush and Ishika. She was a friend, a companion, a love, happiness and a confidant for life for both of them. She was that thread who had kept connected Arush and Ishika even facing a worst phase of their friendship. She was the only reason because of which everything was going right between Arush & Ishika. Arush knew the importance of Aashi in his life. So he wanted to do something very special for her on her birthday.

Arush collected all the pictures of Aashi from her childhood to her college life. Pictures with her family and friends, some of her gorgeous pictures. And planned to put these pictures in sheet in a proper manner with quotation relevant to the pictures just to present each phase of her life beautifully in a sheet. It was really a great idea that can make happy to any girl. But he knew that if he will going to this by himself then he will not able to add that beauty and to add suitable beauty in it he needs the help of creative girl.

The creative girl for Arush was Suhasi, she was his college friend. She agreed to help Arush in making that sheet for Aashi. He explained her everything what to do, but she was a smart girl, didn't take much time to understand the things she need to do. When she completed the sheet she made it even more beautiful than the expectations of Arush. She had decorated the sheet beautifully. Arush give it Ishika in the college before 10 days of her birthday asked Ishika to give it Aashi on her birthday as she was going home on the birthday of her elder sister.

On her birthday, when Aashi seen her gift from Arush she was very happy with that and thanked Arush for that and Arush told her that Suhasi was the who made this beautiful sheet for Aashi.

———◆———

Chapter 24

Was That Really The End...??

Everything was finally going good between them, but its life of Arush so things can't be good for the longer time and a storm came in his life that had finished everything between them.

It was the usual college and one of his friend asked Arush about Ishika. Arush said "She is good". Then he told Arush that he had heard Ishika was dating one of the senior from the college named Varun. This statement by his friend had disturbed him completely, his face was frowned, even though he didn't believed it, but somehow that word "dating" had jolted him. His class friends got the uneasiness on his face and they asked about it from him. Then he told them everything. After that they said "Arush it's true, she had not valued you". Now he was even more shocked that all his friends knew about this.

Well such rumours about Ishika were nothing new; Arush had heard such rumours which relate her with any other boy in school also. But the truth was, she was not interested in anyone, she only bothers for her boyfriend Jatin and no one else. She always clarified that thing to Arush in the school. And he accepted it.

It's a great saying that 'people throw most of the stones on the tree with most tasty fruits, but the quality of fruits on the tree never end with this". Similarly in case of Ishika, she was just like that tree with tasty fruits, because she was the beautiful girl and those rumours were just like the stones that were thrown on tree. But they were never able to put down the dignity of her.

Arush knew that it was just another rumour to put down reputation of Ishika in the college. But Arush still wishing to confirm it once from her because now things had been changed between them. So he immediately asked her to meet him at first she said no but then agreed on the request of Arush.

Arush was not in a proper state of mind that he can talk much to her so he directly asked her "Are you talking to Varun, one of our senior…?"
She said "yes..!!"

Then he asked "Are you dating him..??"

"what…??" she said in a shocking tone.

"I talk to him and Avika knew everything about their chats but there was nothing as you are speaking" she added.

Arush didn't said anything and left from there he was just thinking that why did she mentioned that "Avika knew everything about their chats". Her statement was making him worry and implying that there was something between them. And if not then she didn't clarify him properly. He was in a state of anguish, which simply made him cry.

One of his class friends named Kamya caught him crying and asked him "What happened Arush..?"

"You already know everything.." Arush replied.

"Arush listen, you know Varun is my friend and neighbour and he himself told me that he is dating Ishika and they usually met in café and restaurant outside the college. He even knew about her elder sister and Ishika hadn't told him about her relationship, is she really in a relationship…?" Kamya explained and asked him.

Arush got panic after listening all these and just make Kamya believe about the relationship of Ishika he told her everything about the relationship of Ishika. That was the inexcusable mistake by Arush. He had no right to put someone's personal stuff and previous life in front of anyone. He thought it was demand, the demand of circumstances but that was one of the biggest mistakes of his life.

Arush even said to Kamya that Ishika had just told him that there was nothing as such.

"Arush, you are so innocent, love her so blindly and why will she tell you whether she is with someone or not, you are nothing for her Arush, when she don't even prefer to talk to you, how can you expect that she will tell you truth about this" she explained him.

Somehow her words were justified; there were concern and care for Arush in her words but her words had disturbed him. Things were turned to be worst for him but he can't give up and his last hope was Aashi so he asked Aashi about all this. She told him there was nothing to worry; Ishika & Varun were just friends. And finally Aashi made him felt relaxed and then realized that Varun had just done foolish and cheap act by circulating fake rumours and he got some relief now.

Very next day to that day, Ishika messaged him "Who the hell do you think of yourself? Why don't you just live in your own life? What is the need to always put your nose in my personal stuffs? Why it is always necessary to interfere in my life? I had already tolerated you enough in the school but now no more I want to be happy in my college life that's why I had leave my past behind and also didn't you want in my life but you are just not getting this. What is the need to tell anyone about my relationship, see this is the first and last time I'm warning you to just stay away from me and never ever try to talk to me and if there will be any problem caused in my bond with Avika then I will be never going to forgive you".

Her words were harsh but justified too because she was trying to run away from her past and she was doing it quite well. She was happy with her life and her bond with Avika and she was almost moved on from past but it was Arush who put her past again in front her in her present by disclosing the things about her relationship.

Arush realized his mistake but he just expected that Ishika will once alteast try to understand the circumstances in which Arush had committed that mistake but she didn't and that are how things finished off between them.

Arush thought about those moments that were the best part of his life even its flashback brings tears of happiness in his eyes. He tried to call and message her but she never responded. He starts his each day in a hope that one day she will understand those circumstances in which he committed that mistake.

Well it was all over, but he still loves her and always wishes for her happiness. Arush had packed his bag with lot of beautiful memories related to Ishika and their friendship. He preserved each and every thing related to Ishika because he knew they won't happen again.

And that's how love came in the life of Arush unexpectedly and left him when he started expecting from it. Its not the fault of love but thats the nature of love. Love is not always about to own the person whom you love but sometimes its about just loving selflessly without expecting to own the one whom you love and always going out of the way just for the happiness of that person because loving only the one whom you can own is just like loving yourself...!!!

Hope

I begin my every day with a hope that things will get sought out & we will share the same bond as it was before...,

I hope that one day she will definitely come to me & say "Your care is something which I never want to miss in my life.."

I hope that one day she will say that "Our bond is very special one which I had ever shared with anyone.."

I hope that one day she will say that "I understand what you are going through..",

I hope that one day she will say that "I will be always there for you & she will really mean it"

I hope to be the one who can clear all her doubts so that she will not need anyone else to clear her doubt I hope to be her legend once again...!

These hopes turned to be a dream which never come true as my day ends, but it does not let me to get disappointed because she is the first thought of my every morning, best thought of each day & last thought of every night..."

And these thought let me to illuminate the new day with a new hope...!!

Hope is something that keeps people going during worst time!

May be their togetherness was not there in destiny. But he loves her, cares for her happiness, he just love evertyhing about her, her cute expressions, naughty faces and will always love her because she was the most beautiful person that he had ever found on earth.

He thought of writing a summary about her but when he finished it, it was a book.

"This book is not about the efforts of Arush but it's about the beauty of Ishika, beauty of her heart, beauty of her thoughts that can make any boy to do such efforts just for her happiness ....!!"

www.ingramcontent.com/pod-product-compliance
Lightning Source LLC
Chambersburg PA
CBHW052013240626
47153CB00008B/2852
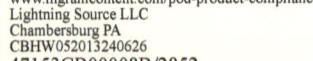